THE GHOSTS OF WESTERN OHIO

Intriguing Tales from
Allen, Auglaize, Champaign, Darke, Mercer, Preble, Shelby, and Warren Counties

Other books by Rita Arnold

Ghosts of Darke County
Ghosts of Darke County II
Ghosts of Darke County III
Ghosts of Darke County IV
The Ghosts Among Us

THE GHOSTS OF WESTERN OHIO

Intriguing Tales from
Allen, Auglaize, Champaign, Darke, Mercer, Preble, Shelby, and Warren Counties

RITA ARNOLD

White Dog Books

ISBN # 0-9788463-0-3
Library of Congress Catalogue

Cover design by Ron D'Allessandris

Printed in the United States of America

Thank you to Keith and Julie at the Darke County Center for the Arts for your continued support.

Please read and enjoy these stories. They were told to me personally by people who want the history and legends of their counties to continue. Their only request was that I do not reveal the exact location of where the events took place.

Many of the locations and names have been changed for their protection. Respect the history and privacy of these areas.

Do you believe in ghosts? You will!

Some Ghosts live here
Some Ghosts live there
But here in Ohio
There are Ghosts everywhere

Some Ghosts live high
Some Ghosts live low
Wherever you find them
They will be on the go.

Milton H. Arnold

Table of Contents

Table of Contents

1.   The Finnarn Livery Ghost

The following is a wonderful story shared by a gentleman whose family has a long history in Darke County.

Since Greenville's beginning in the early 1800's, there has always been "The Circle." This is where Broadway and Main streets cross in the center of town. For years the city building stood in its center and traffic drove carefully around. The clatter of horse and buggies was eventually replaced by the hum of automobiles as they wound around the circle to move toward their destinations.

In the 1950's, following the demolition of the city building, a large decorative water fountain was added. Surrounded by shrubs the year round and flowers in the summer, it continued to be a prominent landmark. The residents often gave directions by saying, "Go to the circle and then follow Broadway north out of town." Not only was the Circle a landmark, but it was also the location of many historical events.

1

One point on the Circle is inhabited by the Municipal Building with the Fire Department next door. Another point is home to several businesses. A third point houses the local post office. On the fourth point stands the Finnarn Law Offices; the location of our story.

In the early 1900's, the Finnarn Livery stood on this spot. The building actually dates back to 1866. At that time, the Fire Department was located next door to the Livery before moving to the present location next to the Municipal Building. Greenville was a growing, busy town, surrounded by prosperous farms and grain mills. Train travel was brisk in Greenville during the late 1800's where farmers brought their produce into town for shipment.

People traveled the streets of this thriving community in their buggies, doing business or attending social events. The livery was often busy stabling the horses and storing or repairing buggies. The livery business was good for its proud owner, Theodore Finnarn, known to his neighbors as Thee. He also was a fireman in the early 1900's. Thee was an integral part of his community and wanted to be active in anyway he could.

Thee, who loved operating his livery was not pleased when the automobile arrived in Greenville. In fact, he operated the last livery in town. He was not shy about his opposition to the motor vehicles that were becoming more popular with each passing day.

Thee Finnarn also served as the Darke County Treasurer for several terms in the 1920's. He was known for campaigning in his horse and buggy throughout the county, always refusing to use an automobile. One sure thing in life is change and, eventually, the livery became a garage and taxi business in spite of Thee's continued opposition to 'mechanized vehicles'.

When Thee passed away in 1949, people who worked at Finnarn Garage (as it was then known), began to notice unusual events. At various times, some of the cab drivers would see a misty, faint, apparition in the back of the building and occasionally just outside the building. Periodically, the taxi drivers saw a horse and buggy being driven past the building only to see it vanish before their eyes. The garage employees could not explain the sound of horses baying, the crack of whips, or the clatter of wagon wheels. Remember, no horses or wagons had been in the building for a number of years. These sounds and sightings would happen on foggy, damp, nights. The employees felt that this was just a sign that Thee was reminding everyone that he felt the value of a horse and buggy was greater than that of an automobile.

Sadly, the building was demolished in 1977-1978 and the location was paved for parking. People walking past this spot on a foggy, damp night would report hearing the noise of wagon wheels, the crack of a whip, and the sound of horses. Some even reported seeing a wagon. But when they took a closer look or tried to locate the source of the sounds, nothing was found. Other people swear they sometimes see the apparition of man standing on the very site of his beloved livery.

In 2006, a new brick structure was erected on the parking lot to house The Finnarn Law Offices. While the building was under construction, the workers often reported hearing the sounds of horses baying, the distinct sound of whips, and the clatter of wagon wheels rolling past. One of the most interesting happenings during the construction was the sighting of wagon wheel tracks in the ground.

Most of the workers did not know the history of this area or the story of Thee disliking of the automobile. When the men stored their tools at the end of their work day, they saw only footprints in the dirt. In the morning, when they returned to their jobs, they often discovered the fresh tracks of wagon wheels.

When the occupants moved into the new building, it was not long before the employees began to notice some strange happenings. In the early evening hours, people looking out the windows would notice a hazy image of a wagon being driven by a man in a long coat and top hat.

Every Christmas season, Greenville has a lighted horse parade that proceeds north on Broadway, around the circle, and then south on Broadway. This parade always has a large number of participants, with thousands of people lining the streets. Many parade goers have reported seeing a hazy, faint apparition of a horse and buggy seeming to be driving proudly in the parade.

It appears that the proud owner of Finnarn's Livery is still intent upon convincing the town that the horse and buggy continues to be the best mode of transportation.

2.   New House – Old Land

On Route 47, just west of Versailles, a house was built in the early 1960's. This was the home of Vernon and Pearlie. They did not design the house, but the minute they walked through during a Sunday afternoon open house they felt right at home. With the added benefit of the surrounding acreage, they quickly decided to purchase the house and raise their children in the country. But, from the very beginning, the family members felt, heard, or saw unusual and unexplainable events.

Pearlie's Uncle Ralph lived just a few houses down the road and visited often. He would always peck gently on the front window with his hand as he walked to the front door. Shortly after his death, a shadow would be seen passing by the window coming from the direction of Uncle Ralph's house. But when a family member opened the front door anticipating the arrival of a guest, no one could be found. As long as Vernon and Pearlie lived in the house, this shadow could be seen passing by the front window. The family felt that Uncle Ralph was still with them.

The inside of the home had its own share of bizarre events. There were often sightings of a man in a dark suit, walking in the hallway toward the bedrooms. He always entered the end bedroom and went straight to the large closet. Vernon always believed this was his brother, Robert. After Robert's death, Vernon inherited his brother's World War I Army uniform. Vernon hung the uniform in the roomier storage in last bedroom. At times, the closet door was seen slowly opening all the way to the door stop with no one near the door. All the way open – not just slightly ajar! Even the door knob would be seen turning on its own! The family believed that Robert was checking on his uniform.

One day in the 1960's, Vernon and Pearlies' son, Johnny, and some of his school buddies decided to watch a movie in the living room. They closed the curtains tightly to block out all of the sun light. As the movie began in the total darkness, one of the boys noticed a small oval shape of light glowing in the corner of the room. There was no light anywhere else. This was the corner nearest the front window where Uncle Ralph would always tap on the glass. Slowly, the light began to move across the wall towards the front door, then down the wall, along the baseboard, and back up to the corner. That was all the boys needed to see and they ran quickly out of the house. One of the boys would never visit inside the house again. Did I mention that Uncle Ralph was shot to death? The sheriff ruled the death a suicide but the family knew better because he was shot in the back with the bullet going straight through his heart.

Pearlie's mother visited often and enjoyed many good meals and good times at her daughter's house. She was often heard to say "how nice." This was her favorite expression if she thought something was pretty or if the food tasted especially good. On the day of her mother's funeral, the clan gathered at Pearlie's house for a family dinner. After the meal was set on the table, some of the family members distinctly heard someone whispering "How nice." Pearlie felt that her mother was, once again, voicing her approval of the meal.

Vernon and Pearlie were never afraid in the house. They enjoyed the feeling that some of their family members were always with them.

RITA ARNOLD

3.   The Bridge

Before the Civil War, canal travel was a popular and convenient method of transportation. One of the most famous canals was the Miami-Erie Canal that wound through the western part of Ohio connecting the Ohio River with Lake Erie. Travel was slow on the canal, but it proved to be an excellent way of moving goods to various markets.

This was the era when the area was mainly agricultural, and towns were small and scattered. The emerging cities were little more than the occasional cluster of a few houses, a general store, and a combination school house and church. The towns, though, were far apart.

The object of this tale is a bridge located just outside of Spencerville. In the 1850's this bridge was a wooden structure that crossed the Miami-Erie Canal. It was not fancy, just wide enough for wagons to cross over the Canal with a slight arch so the canal boats could easily pass under the bridge.

During the hey day of the canal years Bill Jones and Jack Billings made their living by farming and they both enjoyed asking the girls to the local dances or church picnics. As fate would happen, both men fell in love with the same girl – Minnie Warren. For a while, things were civil as Minnie took turns dating each man. When the three of them were all at the same dance, Minnie simply divided her time on the floor between her two partners.

After several months, a rivalry developed between the men for Minnie's hand in marriage. Finally, she made her decision and agreed to marry Jack. Well, before long, Bill's jealousy led to his being overcome with pure hatred for Jack.

On an October night in 1854, Minnie and Jack were walking, home hand-in-hand, from a church harvest dinner. The sun had set a couple of hours earlier and there was a slight chill in the air as the couple approached the bridge. As they neared the middle of the bridge Bill was seen with steel in his eyes, carrying an axe and heading straight for Jack. With one swing of the axe, Bill decapitated his former friend. Minnie, overcome with fright, fainted and fell over the side of the bridge to her death.

Bill turned on his heels and walked into the night never to be seen again. Months later when a local well went dry the owner decided to dig the well deeper hoping to find water. Instead he found a skeleton. The area sheriff identified the remains as Bill Jones. The community could not agree if it was suicide or justice.

Shortly after the murders, an unusual event would occur at the bridge. Every October after sundown, people reported sighting a headless man standing in the middle of the bridge, and he would vanish when approached.

If you cross the bridge on a night with a full moon, stop in the middle and lean over the side. Residents have reported seeing Minnie Warren's face just under the water's surface looking back at the bridge as if she were trying to scream.

When the original bridge was replaced with a modern steel structure, people came from miles around to take a small piece of the old wooden structure. Some of the souvenir seekers reported strange events starting to occur in their houses. Others have no comment.

To this day the bridge is still known as Bloody Bridge. In 1977, the Auglaize County Historical Society erected a marker near the bridge that tells everyone who stops here of the tragic events on that October night.

4.   The Castle

Every town has a well known area or landmark.   In Greenville, Ohio, it is The Circle, in Cincinnati, The Fountain (in downtown), and in Sidney, Ohio, the most famous destination is The Castle.   For John Loughlin, the old saying that "a man's home is his castle," was literally true.

John Loughlin arrived in Sidney, Ohio around 1878 from Cook County, Ireland.   He'd grown up in a working class family and was prepared to work hard in his new and exciting country.   He dreamed of making a really good living and becoming truly successful.

A couple years after arriving in Sidney, John started the Sidney School Furniture Company.   Quickly, his goal of owning a successful business came true as his company experienced rapid growth.   Within a few years, his enterprise was one of the largest manufacturers of excellent wooden school desks in the country.

As befitting a wealthy business owner, he decided to build a new house for his family, and not just any style home would do. He erected a copy of a stone castle from his homeland in Ireland. As John's dream was becoming reality, he was active in every decision including the of selection of the materials. Only the finest cherry, mahogany, walnut, Birdseye maple, and oak lumber were used.

In 1886, the castle was built for the enormous sum of $10,000.00, a figure that stunned the citizens of Sidney as the price of a house. The local residents who were fortunate to work on the house enjoyed telling about the large rooms with high ceilings and the fancy wood trims and moldings. The fireplaces were beyond description.

For years, the residents would walk by just to gaze at the unusual structure. Back then, most people had never seen a picture of a castle, let alone have the opportunity to stand beside an actual structure. Just imagine their amazement at a castle with a turret three stories high and a two story house all built from solid limestone. Only a few residents were fortunate enough to afford a brick home. Most residents owned small houses built from wood. But, no one, except for John Loughlin, had a castle.

Sadly, the aging castle has seen many changes. It has been robbed of all the wonderful wood trims and moldings; the solid cherry staircase is gone, the windows, the doors and their frames are missing, and, of course, the magnificent fireplace mantles are all gone. Only a faint outline of where the mantles once stood still remains. And in place of the once beautiful staircase, is a large hole. Only the memories remain. Or not.

As you walk past this location in the fall on a cool, moonlit night, it is said you will hear the soft sound of crying in the distance, but you will find no earthly person. Then there are times when you approach the area that the vision of a man is seen standing on the sidewalk staring at the house. He never moves – just stands still staring at his home. As you get closer to the image, the vision suddenly vanishes. Is this the ghost of John Loughlin yearning for his beautiful castle?

RITA ARNOLD

5. Another Bridge

I was invited to tell ghost stories to a club in West Alexandria, Ohio a few years ago. The audience was composed of all ages and everyone had a great time. Of course, the fact that a thunder storm raged outside in the dark made for a perfect October night

After the meeting, many of the attendees came up to me to express their thanks for a fun time on a dreary night. I noticed one lady hanging back from the crowd, though, for what reason, I was unsure.

As I started to gather my things to head home, she approached me and said her name was Linda. She insisted that she had to tell me a story but only with the promise that I not use her last name. Here is the story as Linda remembers it, from her youth.

Linda was in her late thirties and grew up near Gratis, Ohio. On one of the township roads outside of Gratis was an old bridge built in 1887 that crossed Sam's Run Creek. The bridge was constructed like most bridges from the period, built of wood with open sides and covered with a solid wood roof. There was no electricity at that time so crossing the bridge at night was difficult and dangerous.

In the early 1920's, agricultural town activities would center on the church or the grange. The grange would hold various gatherings for the town, and the most popular for the young people were the dances. That was their chance to socialize and have some fun. Remember, in those days most young people helped on the family farm or worked at the family business while attending school. Naturally, they would always look forward to a dance – their opportunity to hang out with their peers.

In those days, teenagers did not own their cars since only a very few of their parents had an automobile. So, naturally, if a young man was driving his father's car, everyone wanted a ride – especially the girls. Since the car in this story was a convertible, the young driver had packed it full of his friends.

Linda told of an automobile full of teenagers was heading down the road towards the bridge. No one was sure exactly what happened but the car wrecked inside the dark and narrow bridge just before exiting. Due to the tremendous impact with the bridge itself, the passengers were thrown in all directions on the road and into the water. A couple of the boys stood up in a daze and wandered to the edge of the creek, only to fall in and drown.

One of the girls crawled away from the wreck on her hands and knees. With blood running into her eyes from a serious head injury, she crawled towards the road. Unfortunately, she was headed, instead, in the direction of the creek. When she reached the edge of the creek she fell - face first - into the mud and suffocated.

By the time help arrived, there were several deaths and many severe injuries to be attended to by any able person who could help. A couple of men noticed something in the water and pulled out the body of a young boy.

The teenagers were buried and the survivors grieved, but life had to continue. For one family, life was very difficult because after weeks of searching the creek and the surrounding area, they never found their son. With heavy hearts, the family decided to move west and to try to start a new life.

A few years after the tragic accident, the creek was very low due to a severe drought. At a point where the creek bent to the right were a few large boulders. It was here that a couple of young boys who wanted to try some fishing made a gruesome discovery. They found a body.

The boys ran for their fathers who then summoned the local sheriff. He identified the body as being the boy whose family had moved west. Eventually the boy's body was reunited with his family. Or maybe not.

If you park your car along the creek just before entering the bridge after the sun has set on a quiet still night, you might be in for something unusual. There have been reportings of a tapping sound on car windows as if someone were trying to get your attention. Some have reported that when they drove through the bridge, their car engine died.

Are the sounds still there? Let's just say Linda has not been near that bridge in years and has no plans to visit it in the future.

6.   Strange Sights

The area between Camden, West Alexandria, and Eaton, Ohio is full of some interesting tales. There is documentation that in the late 1700's and very early 1800's Native Americans lived here.

In the 1780's and 1790's soldiers were sent to this area to chase out the Indians and make this location safe for the immigration of the white man. A series of forts was built by soldiers in western Ohio on what is now called the Ohio River North to the Lake Erie area.

Locals have reported seeing a soldier, dressed in a uniform from the 1700's, and marching near where Fort St. Clair was located. The soldier vanishes when people try to get close to him. They have also reported seeing a Native American dancing around a campfire in a gulley a few miles away from the fort, but they never hear a sound or smell any smoke from the campfire.

No one knows if these sightings are related, but they have been seen by many throughout the years; and, always in the early evenings.

There is an old school, no longer in use, outside of a town on Route 503. It just stands empty and lonely. The building is surrounded with farm land with just a few houses scattered nearby.

Many people claim to have seen ghostly figures, illuminated by mysterious lights, moving in the fields surrounding the school. These apparitions appear to be marching in line or dancing in a circle, but they quickly vanished when approached. Some residents have even reported hearing voices or the sound of laughter emanating from these figures.

Some people feel that because this was a battleground, that some of the soldiers and the Native Americans are still here.

No one has been harmed by these apparitions. In fact, when people tell me about these sightings they seem happy to have witnessed such occurrences. Could it be that these events remind people of the history of the area and the hardships endured by the early settlers?

7.   Haunted House

The following is a story about a house torn down years and years ago. It was located near Celina, Ohio, not far from Grand Lake St. Mary's. The old legend is that the house was haunted for years before being demolished and to this day the ghosts still roam the area.

The Arnold family had a large fortune; in fact, no one remembers a time when the family was not wealthy. The parents died of natural causes within a couple of years of each other. Their three adult children inherited the wealth. The two married sons each received ten percent and the spinster daughter received the remaining eighty percent of the fortune.

Why the estate was divided this way was never explained, but the town's citizens all knew that the daughter was the smartest one of the children. She had the brains to run the family business. The two sons were playboys. Yes, they were married, but it was common knowledge that the sons enjoyed the ladies.

A short time after their parent's death, the sons had spent all of their inheritance and asked their sister for more money. She refused because she wanted to honor her parents will and was disgusted with her brothers' restless life styles.

As often happens, money can lead to jealousy, and the two brothers soon decided to plot their sister's demise. Finally, the opportunity presented itself and the brothers poisoned their sister and threw her body into the farm's well. The oldest son inherited the majority of the money, but the youngest son quickly became extremely jealous and decided to kill his older brother.

One day the brothers were both in the farm's slaughter house when the younger man achieved his current goal by bludgeoning his brother to death with an axe. After a few days had passed, the man could not live with himself and a few weeks later he was found hanging from a rafter in the barn. He committed suicide, or so the authorities ruled at the time.

With one exception, the family is again all together, only now it is in the family cemetery surrounded by a wrought iron fence. The family was very devout to its Catholic faith (with some detours in life) and because the belief of the day was mortal sinners could not be buried with their family, the youngest son was therefore buried outside the family plot in an isolated area.

The family farm was sold at sheriff's auction to a family new to the area. When they learned of the history of the previous owners, the husband and wife both said that did not matter. They would be very happy in their new home. A couple of years later the house was again up for sale, and this pattern continued until finally the house was abandoned, to stand alone in the weather, with no one to care for it.

As the years passed the area residents would occasionally stop and look in the windows, admiring the hand carved fireplaces, the fancy wood doors, the maple and oak inlay in the foyer, and the fine hand crochet seen on the backs of the chairs and couch.

The interesting part was that the house was never dusty, in spite of its country location. The fancy carved wood baluster on the winding stairway was always brightly polished. It was well known that the sister kept a spotless house as well as working hard at the family business and the farm. The only curtains still hanging in the house were in the north window in the sister's bedroom that she used her entire life; the room where she was poisoned by her brothers.

There were days when the curtains would be parted as if to allow the sunlight into the room. For years people were sure that they saw a woman's face in the bedroom window. But if they looked too hard and long, the face would fade away. Over the years the curtains never faded or fell apart.

As long as the barn stood, people would look in the wide south doorway and swear that they saw a rope hanging from the rafter. The rope was pulled taunt as if a heavy weight was hanging from it and it swung slowly back and forth, back and forth.

If you wandered into the old slaughter house you would see an interesting sight. On the walls about six to eight feet above the floor were blood stains, much too high to be the result of animals being slaughtered. And on one wall was an axe mark at the six foot level – the same height as a man.

THE GHOSTS OF WESTERN OHIO

Years ago someone decided that the well should be filled in for safety reasons. Just before the work began, one of the workers looked into the well and let out a loud scream! He jumped back and told his buddies to run. After telling his friends that he saw a man's face in the well staring up at him, none of them wanted to hang around. Finally everyone settled down and the men decided to just cover the well and get out of there.

For decades, people have reported hearing cries and moans in the vicinity of the old well. If you get too close, you may think that you hear a man shouting.

No one has lived in the house for years, and no one spends much time walking around the farm. Could it be respect for the once wealthy and prosperous family or is it because the Arnold's are still there?

Rita Arnold

8.   The Convent

In the late 1800's and into the first half of the 1900's, various Catholic churches, seminaries, and convents were built in western Ohio. Many of them were located outside of small towns to minister to the citizens of the area and to take advantage of the inexpensive land.

The church could buy a good size farm and be self sufficient. Local farmers rented some of the acreage and the church used the rent money for its mission work.

In the 1850's, the Catholic Church bought some farm land outside of St. Marys, Ohio. Even in the 1800's this land was reported to be haunted. Strange sounds could be heard at night such as the voices of people talking and laughing, or the sound of a wagon pulled by a team of horses. Others reports the smell of a cooking fire.

For years, lights were seen moving across the land as if someone were carrying a lantern and walking across the open field. In the late 1700's Native Americans were living here and around that time the American soldiers started coming to this area to build forts and to encourage the eastern population to move westward.

This particular area of land stood unused for years. No one farmed the land and no one would hunt in this location. People just tried to ignore the sounds and sights of this unusual farm land.

Undoubtedly, some of the residents laughed when the Church bought the land. Others were happy about the convent locating into their area. What a good influence for the young people. And who could complain about having a convent for a neighbor? Many looked forward to having the shrine built.

For years the convent thrived. The farm was prosperous and the convent residents seem to enjoy the farm and the trips to surrounding towns.

Time passed and the administrator of the shrine, Sister Maria, passed away in the 1960's. On the day that she died all of the sisters and the employees of the shrine gathered in the chapel to pray. It was a sunny day and the light brought the stain glass windows to life.

As evening approached, some of the town's people joined the gathering in the chapel. Suddenly, the chapel lights went out, followed a few seconds later by a flash of light. A round ball of light was seen a couple of minutes later slowly rising toward heaven from above the shrine. Many in the chapel strongly believed that this light was Sister Maria on her final journey.

Was it a faulty transformer, electrical wiring going bad, or was it Sister Maria?

RITA ARNOLD

9.   The Gorge

In the early 1800's, when our country was being developed, the settlers followed one of five major trails heading westward. Think about the people traveling in wagons, on horse back, or walking along the trail heading into unknown territory. People were living on hopes and dreams to find the Promised Land. Many dreamed of that special farm land or the opportunity to start a business.

There was not much consideration or thought given to the people who were already occupying the lands – the American Indian. The Indians had lived on and with these lands for hundreds of years and this sudden and large influx of people was difficult to understand. Over the years thousands of people traveled this trail, some stopping in eastern Ohio, others moving on to the western Ohio territories and beyond. At that time, Western Ohio was thought of as "the Wild West."

The Indians were gradually being pushed from the lands where they lived and hunted. This western Ohio area was thickly wooded and rich with wildlife. Some of the settlers decided to head north of the trail to claim land in what is now Darke County, Ohio. Others headed south into Preble County, Ohio.

Our story takes place in an area outside of Camden, Ohio. Here the land rolls and dips, making a very scenic drive. To the Native Americans, it also provided a wonderful area for hunting.

As the white man moved in and took over the land, tempers flared and soon fighting developed between the settlers and the Native Americans. As the number of settlers increased over the years, the fighting became more intense and the number of Native Americans grew to large numbers as various tribes joined forces to defend there land.

After one particularly ferocious battle along a gorge, the Native Americans lost their revered leaders. This was devastating to the Indians who soon left the area to decide what to do. The population of the Indians had decreased greatly. Realizing that they were significantly outmanned, they decided to head west, hoping to avoid any further contact with the white man.

Before leaving the territory, the Indians tried to retrieve the bodies of their fallen leaders but the settlers fought off every attempt. Chief Red Turtle is said to have cursed the area in one of his last acts before leaving the land that he loved.

Do you believe in curses? Deaths of any settlers by unknown causes in the early 1800's would be blamed on the Native American ghosts. It was believed that the ghosts of the fallen leaders would prowl the area and seek revenge. To this very day, area residents believe that the ghosts are still in the area, watching the settlers.

People walking the gorge at night will hear soft footsteps behind them in the thickly forested area. No one is ever seen, but people do feel as if they are being watched.

Some people have reported finding evidence of campfires near the gorge but with no indication of people having hiked to the location.

In this area, a woman hung herself after her infant suddenly died. If you stand near the hanging tree and softly say, "Mama, mama, mama," you will hear a baby cry in the distance; the cry of a baby wanting help.

Another interesting piece of information about this area is the fact that there have been Bigfoot sightings here as recently as the 1970's. But that is another story and another book. Watch for it!

10. The Town

I love talking with residents of small towns, especially the people who have lived in that town or county for years and years. These are the people who know the history and legends of a location. They have seen the changes that affected their lives and how they lived. Remember some of the small towns were among the last in the nation to benefit from changes in technology, such as telephones, electricity, and paved roads.

I remember my grandmother, who lived on a farm outside of town (a population of 80), talking about when electricity first came into the area, the house with the first and only telephone for a few years, and the big excitement of the first paved road. Also, I remember hearing the stories of the local characters and the legends that continue to live in the minds of people.

Older residents of any community remember not just the facts about some local historical events but the characters involved. These stories never get printed in the history books or become documented in the local historical museums. These are the people I enjoy getting to know.

Warren County, Ohio, is home to the beautiful town of Waynesville. This town has retained the character and charm of a by-gone era. Certainly, there are plenty of new houses being constructed, in everything from contemporary to the old colonial style. New commercial buildings have been built in recent years for gas stations, groceries, and other businesses and the school system continues to provide modern buildings for the children. These are excellent signs that the community is keeping up with progress.

The heart of the old downtown area is where the time worn buildings remain. These are the structures from the 1800's and the early 1900's that I wish could talk to me. In fact, sometimes I think old buildings do speak to us if we just stop and listen. Turn off the radio and television, stop text messaging and listen to the old buildings as they creak and groan.

Louisa lived in her family home in Waynesville in the late 1860's. She never married, making her living as the town seamstress, and was also well respected for her church work.

One summer her brother, John, came to visit. Following his the long journey, he arrived thoroughly exhausted with a bad cough. He thought it was due to the long, bitter-cold winter in the east where he had his law practice. Thinking that a few weeks with his sister would be relaxing and the change of climate would be good for his health, he left New England for Ohio.

Later that summer John's health was still not improving but he decided to return home to his law practice, hoping the work would do him some good.

Sadly, after he left Waynesville, Louisa became ill. Her doctor diagnosed her illness as tuberculosis which, in the 1870's, had no cure. The local physician treated her as best he could but Louisa died one evening quietly in her home in 1879.

For years after her death the house was used as a residence and then as a commercial building for an antique business. The only major change was the complete removal of the kitchen to allow more space for inventory, yet the smell of baking gingerbread pervades throughout the building. Louisa was famous for her gingerbread!

There are other unexplained events that are reported to take place in this building. For example, as people walk along the sidewalk near the house, they claim to see the vision of a dark-haired woman dressed in old-fashion clothing standing at a window, Also, any mirrors hanging on the walls during the day are always removed by some unknown hand during the night and carefully placed on the floor. The mirrors are never broken.

Finally, if there were any sewing items in the building, they were mysteriously rearranged. Were these items moved by Louisa, the seamstress, as if she were about to begin a sewing project?

11.   The Patrol Car

Like many counties in this area, Allen County has an old narrow bridge with a legend connected to it. This is a story that has continued to be told for years and years.

There is no documentation that the following event truly happened, but the legend is that many years ago, a carload of teenagers died on this bridge. The car either stalled on the bridge or developed some type of engine trouble. No one remembers if the teenagers died in a strange accident or were murdered. Supposedly their bodies were scattered along the bridge with one of them hung over a stop sign. The legend is the stop sign bleeds at night! The sign has been replaced a number of times and supposedly still continues to bleed.

A few years ago some teenagers decided to drive across the bridge at nighttime because they wanted to check out the legend. The stop sign did not bleed but -

After driving across the bridge a couple of times, the driver stopped the car on the third pass and rolled down the windows. Hearing nothing but silence one of the teens yelled out, "Anyone here?" After a few minutes, a car drove up behind them with its headlights flashing.

The teens immediately drove off the bridge only to be followed by the car. Soon the car behind them turned on overhead flashing lights and the teens realized that it was a police car and the officer wanted them to stop.

Because they were driving on an old, skinny country roadway the teens drove until they could pull into a farm lane to stop. The police car stopped behind them and the patrolman approached the car.

Before the policeman could speak, a county sheriff's car stopped near by. Suddenly the first policeman and his car vanished! Excitedly the teens jumped out of their car and started talking all at once to the deputy sheriff. After calming the teens down he pieced together the events of the evening. Then he informed them that there were no other police near the scene when he arrived.

The deputy sheriff knew some of the teens personally and understood that they were just out for fun and hoping to find a ghost. The teens knew that something special had happened because the vanishing patrol car was green and no one in that area used green patrol cars. The model and paint style of the green patrol car was from years ago.

RITA ARNOLD

12.   Interesting Stories

I spoke one evening to small group of senior citizens in Champaign County telling some of my ghost stories and listening to theirs. Most of the audience had lived in the county their entire lives and were very familiar with the local legends. The following tales provided me with great enjoyment. I hope you, too, will be equally enthralled.

Like most counties in Ohio, Champaign County has a location known as Crybaby Bridge. This particular bridge crosses over a couple of railroad tracks. Years ago these tracks were busy with almost constant train traffic.

One fall evening a very young unmarried girl stood on the highest point of the bridge looking down at the tracks. It was an era that if an unmarried girl became pregnant she was sent away from home until she "recovered from her condition."

No one remembers the young girl's name. They just recall the fact that she was not married and was holding a tiny baby in her arms. She stood like a statue staring down at the tracks waiting, waiting. Soon in the distance the whistle of an approaching train was heard. Still she continued to stand on the bridge waiting, waiting.

Suddenly, just before the approaching train started under the bridge the young girl jumped with her baby tightly held in her arms to their immediate deaths. She screamed and held her baby to the very end.

If you drive your car across the bridge during the fall do not be surprised if it stalls at the highest point. Roll down your car window and listen. Soon, you will hear the distant sound of a train whistle, followed by the cry of a baby and the scream of a woman. Do not be afraid because, as you look around, you will see no train, no baby, and no woman.

Now, your car will start and you may continue your journey.

There is a cemetery in Champaign County that has a most unusual tombstone – it glows. No one knows much about the person buried at this site, and no one knows anything about the type of stone that was used for the marker.

Some residents think the marker has some kind of phosphorescent fungus on it that reflects light from passing cars. But how do you explain the fact that it glows with no cars on the nearby roadway? As for the fungus theory, people have used many different cleaners and polishes; but still the marker continues to glow.

The local residents like to think of it as a haunted grave and the deceased person is just keeping an eye on everything.

Everyone knows that Abraham Lincoln's body traveled by train from Washington, D.C. back to Illinois. The funeral train made several stops along the way so the American citizens could pay their final respects. Some of the stops were only for a few minutes so people could look at the train car containing the casket surrounded by soldiers at each corner.

The train made one of the short stops in Champaign County before continuing its journey to Illinois.

The legend is that during April along a certain location, people can stand quietly along the train tracks and see the funeral train slowly come to a stop. The train cars are draped in black, the coffin is guarded by four soldiers in full civil war uniforms, but these particular soldiers are just skeletons still at attention. After a very short stop, the train moves on without making a sound.

Clocks in the surrounding area will stop when the vision appears and restart only when the train leaves. These clocks are then found to be about five to ten minutes late.

In a small town, in this county, is an old house that is nearing collapse due to vandalism and neglect. The house was in the process of being built by the owner himself when the man's wife and children were killed in a tragic train wreck.

The husband was so distraught that he could not continue to live without his much loved family and hung himself one night from the huge oak tree in the front yard.

Now when people walk past the house they will hear unusual sounds. Sometimes the sounds of hammering and sawing are heard, at other times they hear the soft wailing of a man crying. Occasionally, in the evening, people will see a man hanging from the oak tree, but as they approach the tree the man vanishes right before their eyes.

RITA ARNOLD

13.   The Drowning

Greenville Creek meanders through town in a crooked lazy way that provides some beautiful scenes. The creek is lined with huge old trees and flows toward the center of town toTecumseh Point where the Treaty of Greenville was signed.

With the coming of Spring's heavy rains, the creek will rise quite high and make for some good rafting. Years ago young boys could be seen riding home- made wooden rafts down the creek, laughing and having fun.

In the late 1800's Jerry and one of his friends, unknown to their parents, met at the creek for a Sunday morning of rafting. Both boys had a paddle with Jerry sitting up front on the raft and his buddy behind him. The boys talked for awhile and then lapsed into comfortable silence, enjoying their ride on the creek.

After awhile, Jerry said something to his buddy. When he heard no answer Jerry turned around only to discover that his friend was gone!

Jerry never heard a splash, there were no ripples in the water, and Jerry did not see a body floating in the water. He quickly became scared, jumped off the raft and swam toward the shore. He raced into town screaming for help. Crying and choking with despair he finally told some people the story about what had just happened.

Everyone raced down to the creek looking for Jerry's buddy. After hours of searching the creek and the surrounding area, the people gave up. A couple of days later, there was a memorial services for the missing boy.

Jerry was so distraught that he ran away from home the following week. He lived a lonely life; stealing, begging, or working for food. Being a young boy, Jerry kept on the move not wanting the authorities to find him. He just could not face the people back in Greenville.

One night Jerry was sleeping in a small cave he found in some woods. He fell asleep thinking about his buddy. Jerry always said his prayers at night just like his mother taught him. He hoped for forgiveness and prayed for his buddy's family. This one night he heard a soft voice calling him – "Jerry, Jerry, you know me Jerry." Jerry jumped up and asked "where are you?" The voice answered, "I'm home now Jerry, you go back to your home. Your family needs you. They miss you."

The next morning Jerry began his long journey and, eventually, arrived safely back home.

After years had passed, Jerry often thought about that night in the cave when he heard the voice. He was sure that it was his buddy advising him to go back home. Jerry's mother believed it was God telling Jerry to return home.

For years after the accident, people thought that they saw the body of a young boy floating in the water. This would always happen on an early Sunday morning when people walked across the bridge or along a certain spot in the creek. By the time they had raced down to the creek bank, nothing could be found. No log or debris was seen floating in the water.

Jerry returned to Greenville to live out his life but he never returned to the Greenville Creek. He heard the stories of the sightings but never went near the creek.

Now that you have read the book,

It's time to say adieu,

Think of the friendly ghost,

That will be watching over you.

Milton H. Arnold